THE FLOWERED THUNDERMUG

MORE WILDSIDE CLASSICS

THE FLOWERED THUNDERMUG

ALFRED BESTER

THE FLOWERED THUNDERMUG

Originally published in Alfred Bester's 1964 collection of short stories, *The Dark Side of the Earth*. Never copyrighted.

This edition published in 2008 by Wildside Press, LLC.
www.wildsidebooks.com

"We will conclude this first semester of Antiquities 107," Professor Paul Muni said, "with a reconstruction of an average day in the life of a mid-twentieth-century inhabitant of the United States of America, as Great L.A. was known five hundred years ago.

"Let us refer to him as Jukes, one of the proudest names of the times, immortalized in the Kallikak-Jukes-feud sagas. It is now generally agreed that the mysterious code letters JU, found in the directories of Hollywood East, or New York City as it was called then — viz., JU 6-0600 or JU 2-1914 — indicate in some manner a genealogical relationship to the powerful Jukes dynasty.

"The year is 1950. Mr. Jukes, a typical 'loner' — i.e., 'bachelor' — lives on a small ranch outside New York. He rises at dawn, dresses in spurred boots, Daks slacks, rawhide shirt, gray flannel waistcoat and black knit tie. He arms himself with a Police Positive revolver or a Frontier Six Shooter and goes out to the Bar-B-Q to prepare his breakfast of curried plankton or converted algae. He may or may not surprise juvenile delinquents or red Indians on his ranch in the act of lynching a victim or rustling his automobiles, of which he has a herd of perhaps one hundred and fifty.

"These hooligans he disperses after single combat with his fists. Like all twentieth-century Americans, Jukes is a brute of fantastic strength, giving and receiving sledgehammer blows, or being battered by articles of furniture with inexhaustible resilience. He rarely uses his gun on such occasions; it is usually reserved for ceremonial rituals.

"Mr. Jukes journeys to his job in New York City on horseback; in a sports car (a kind of open automobile), or on an electric trolley car. He reads his morning newspaper, which will feature such stories as: 'The Discovery of the North Pole,' 'The Sinking of the Luxury Liner Titanic,' 'The Successful Orbiting of Mars by Manned Space Capsule,' or 'The Strange Death of President Harding.'

"Jukes works in an advertising agency situated on Madison

Avenue (now Sunset Boulevard East), which, in those days, was a rough muddy highway, traversed by stagecoaches, lined with gin mills and populated by bullies, corpses and beautiful nightclub performers in abbreviated dresses. Jukes is an agency man, dedicated to the guidance of taste, the improvement of culture, the election of public officers and the selection of national heroes.

"His office on the twentieth floor of a towering skyscraper is decorated in the characteristic style of the mid-twentieth century. He has a roll-top desk, a Null-G, or Free Fall chair and a brass spittoon. Illumination is by Optical Maser light pumps. Large fans suspended from the ceiling cool him in the summer, and an infrared Franklin stove warms him in the winter.

"The walls are decorated with rare pictures executed by such famous painters as Michelangelo, Renoir and Sunday. Alongside the desk is a tape recorder, which he uses for dictation. His words are later written down by a secretary using a pen and carbon ink. (It has, by now, been clearly demonstrated that the typewriting machine was not developed until the onset of the Computer Age at the end of the twentieth century.)

"Mr. Jukes's work involves the creation of the spiritual slogans that uplift the consumer half of the nation. A few of these have come down to us in more or less fragmentary condition, and those of you who have taken Professor Rex Harrison's course, Linguistics 916, know the extraordinary difficulties we are encountering in our attempts to interpret: 'Good to the Last Drop' (for 'good' read 'God'?); 'Does She or Doesn't She?' (what?); and 'I Dreamed I Went to the Circus in My Maidenform Bra' (incomprehensible).

"At midday, Mr. Jukes takes a second meal, usually a community affair with thousands of others in a giant stadium. He returns to his office and resumes work, but you must understand that conditions were not ideal for concentration, which is why he was forced to labor as much as four and six hours a day. In those deplorable times there was a constant uproar of highway robberies, hijackings, gang wars and other brutalities. The air was filled with falling bodies as despairing brokers leaped from their office windows.

"Consequently it is only natural for Mr. Jukes to seek spiritual peace at the end of the day. This he finds at a ritual called a 'cocktail party.' He and many other believers stand close-packed in a small room, praying aloud, and filling the air with the sacred residues of marijuana and mescaline. The women worshipers often wear vestments called 'cocktail dresses,' otherwise known as 'basic black.'

"Afterward, Mr. Jukes may take his last meal of the day in a night club, an underground place of entertainment where rare shows are presented. He is often accompanied by his 'expense account,' a phrase difficult to interpret. Dr. David Niven argues most cogently that it was cant for 'a woman of easy virtue,' but Professor Nelson Eddy points out that this merely compounds the difficulty, since no one today knows what 'a woman of easy virtue' was.

"Finally, Mr. Jukes returns to his ranch on a 'commuters' special,' a species of steam car, on which he plays games of chance with the professional gamblers who infested all the transportation systems of the times At home, he builds a small outdoor fire, calculates the day's expenses on his abacus, plays sad music on his guitar, makes love to one of the thousands of strange women who made it a practice of intruding on campfires at odd hours, rolls up in a blanket and goes to sleep.

"Such was the barbarism of that age — an age so hysteric that few men lived beyond one hundred years. And yet romantics today yearn for that monstrous era of turmoil and terror. Twentieth-century Americana is all the vogue. Only recently, a single copy of Life, a sort of mail-order catalogue, was bought at auction by the noted collector Clifton Webb for $150,000. I might mention, in passing, that in my analysis of that curio in the current Phil. Trans. I cast grave doubts on its authenticity. Certain anachronisms in the text indicate a possible forgery.

"And now a final word about your term examinations. There has been some talk about bias on the part of the computer. It has been suggested that when this department took over the Multi-III from Biochemistry, various circuits were overlooked and left operative, prejudicing the computer in favor of the mathematical approach. This is utter nonsense. Our computer psychiatrist assures me that the Multi-III was completely brainwashed and reindoctrinated. Exhaustive checks have shown that all errors were the result of student carelessness.

"I urge you to observe the standard sterilization procedures before taking your examination. Do not scamp your wash-up. Make sure your surgical caps, gowns, masks and gloves are properly adjusted. Be certain that your punching tools are in register and sterile. Remember that one speck of contamination on your answer card can wreck your results. The Multi-III is not a machine, it is a brain, and requires the same care and consideration you give your own bodies. Thank you, good luck, and I hope to see you all again next semester."

Coming out of the lecture hall, Professor Muni was met in the crowded corridor by his secretary, Ann Sothern. She was wearing a polka dot bikini, carried a tray of drinks and had a pair of the professor's swim trunks draped over her arm. Muni nodded in appreciation, swallowed a quick one and frowned at the traditional musical production number with which the students moved from class to class. He began reassembling his lecture notes as they hurried from the building.

"No time for a dip, Miss Sothern," he said. "I'm scheduled to sneer at a revolutionary discovery in the Medical Arts Building this afternoon."

"It's not on your calendar, Dr. Muni."

"I know. I know. But Raymond Massey is sick, and I'm standing in for him. Ray says he'll substitute for me the next time I'm due to advise a young genius to give up poetry."

They left the Sociology Building, passed the teardrop swimming pool, the book-shaped library, the heart-shaped Heart Clinic, and came to the faculty-shaped Faculty-Building. It was in a grove of royal palms through which a miniature golf course meandered, its air conditioners emitting a sibilant sound. Inside the Faculty Building, concealed loudspeakers were broadcasting the latest noise-hit.

"What is it — Caruso's 'Niagara'?" Professor Muni asked absently.

"No, Callas's 'Johnstown Flood,'" Miss Sothern answered, opening the door of Muni's office. "Why, that's odd. I could have sworn I left the lights on." She felt for the light switch.

"Stop," Professor Muni snapped. "There's more here than meets the eye, Miss Sothern."

"You mean . . . ?"

"Who does one traditionally encounter on a surprise visit in a darkened room? I mean, whom."

"Th-the Bad Guys?"

"Precisely."

A nasal voice spoke. "You are so right, my dear professor, but I assure you this is purely a private business matter."

"Dr. Muni," Miss Sothern gasped. "There's someone in your office."

"Do come in, professor," the nasal voice said. "That is, if you will permit me to invite you into your own office. There is no use trying to turn on the lights, Miss Sothern. They have been — attended to."

"What is the meaning of this intrusion?" Professor Muni demanded.

"Come in. Come in. Boris, guide the professor to a chair. The goon who is taking your arm, Professor Muni, is my ruthless bodyguard, Boris Karloff. I am Peter Lorre."

"I demand an explanation," Muni shouted. "Why have you invaded my office? Why are the lights out? By what right do you —"

"The lights are out because it is best that people do not see Boris. He is a most useful man, but not, shall we say, an aesthetic delight. Why I have invaded your office will be made known to you after you have answered one or two trifling questions."

"I will do nothing of the sort. Miss Sothern, get the dean."

"You will remain where you are, Miss Sothern."

"Do as you're told, Miss Sothern. I will not permit this —"

"Boris, light something."

Something was lit. Miss Sothern screamed. Professor Muni was dumb-struck.

"All right, Boris, put it out. Now, my dear professor, to business. First, let me inform you that it will be worth your while to answer my questions honestly. Be good enough to put out your hand." Professor Muni extended his hand. A sheaf of bills was placed in it. "Here is one thousand dollars; your consultation fee. Would you care to count it? Shall I have Boris light something?"

"I believe you," Muni muttered.

"Very good. Professor Muni, where and how long did you study American history?"

"That's an odd question, Mr. Lorre."

"You have been paid, Professor Muni."

"Very true. Well . . . I studied at Hollywood High, Harvard High, Yale High and the College of the Pacific."

"What is 'college'?"

"The old name for a high. They're traditionalists at Pacific — hidebound reactionaries."

"And how long did you study?"

"Some twenty years."

"How long have you been teaching here at Columbia High?"

"Fifteen years."

"Then that adds up to thirty-five years of experience. Would you say that you had an extensive knowledge of the merits and qualifications of the various living historians?"

"Fairly extensive. Yes."

"Then who, in your opinion, is the leading authority on twentieth-century Americana?"

"Ah. So. Very interesting. Harrison, of course, on advertising copy, newspaper headlines, and photo captions. Taylor on domestic science — that's Dr. Elizabeth Taylor. Gable is probably your best bet for transportation. Clark's at Cambridge High now, but he —"

"Excuse me, Professor Muni. I put the question badly. I should have asked: Who is the leading authority on twentieth-century objects of virtu? Antiques, paintings, furniture, curios, objets d'art, and so forth . . ."

"Ah! I have no hesitation in answering that, Mr. Lorre. Myself."

"Very good. Very good. Now listen carefully, Professor Muni. I have been delegated by a little group of powerful men to hire your professional services. You will be paid ten thousand dollars in advance. You will give your word that the transaction will be kept secret. And it must be understood that if your mission fails, we will do nothing to help you."

"That's a lot of money," Professor Muni said slowly. "How can I be sure that this offer is from the Good Guys?"

"You have my assurance that it is for freedom and justice, the man on the street, the underdogs and the L.A. Way of Life. Of course, you can refuse this dangerous assignment, and it will not be held against you, but you are the one man in all Great L.A. who can carry it out."

"Well," Professor Muni said, "seeing that I have nothing better to do than mistakenly sneer at a cancer cure today, I might as well accept."

"I knew we could depend on you. You are the sort of little man that makes L.A. great. Boris, sing the national anthem."

"Thank you, but I need no praise. I'm just doing what any loyal, red-blooded, one-hundred-percent Angelino would do."

"Very good. I will pick you up at midnight. You will be wearing rough tweeds, a felt hat pulled down over your face and stout shoes. You will carry one hundred feet of mountaineering rope, prism binoculars and an ugly snub-nosed fission gun. Your code identity will be .369."

"This," Peter Lorre said, "is .369. .369, may I have the pleasure of introducing you to X, Y and Z?"

"Good evening, Professor Muni," the Italian-looking gentleman said. "I am Vittorio De Sica. This is Miss Garbo. That is Edward Everett Horton. Thank you, Peter. You may go."

Mr. Lorre exited. Muni stared around. He was in a sumptuous penthouse apartment decorated entirely in white. Even the fire burning in the grate was, by some miracle of chemistry, composed entirely of milk-white flames. Mr. Horton was pacing nervously before the fire. Miss Garbo reclined languidly on a polar-bear skin, an ivory cigarette holder drooping from her hand.

"Let me relieve you of that rope, professor," De Sica said. "And the customary binoculars and snub-nosed pistol, I presume? I'll take them too. Do make yourself comfortable. You must forgive our being in faultless evening dress; our cover identities, you understand. We operate the gambling hell downstairs. Actually we are —"

"No!" Mr. Horton cried in alarm.

"Unless we have full faith in Professor Muni and are perfectly candid, we will get nowhere, my dear Horton. You agree, Greta?" Miss Garbo nodded.

"Actually," De Sica continued, "we are a little group of powerful art dealers."

Muni stammered, "Th-then . . . Then you're the De Sica, and the Garbo, and the Horton?"

"We are."

"B-but . . . But everyone says you don't exist. Everyone believes that the organization known as the Little Group of Powerful Art Dealers is really owned by 'The Thirty-nine Steps,' with the controlling interest vested in Cosa Vostro. It is said that —"

"Yes, yes," De Sica interrupted. "That is what we desire to have believed; hence our cover identity as the sinister trio operating this gambling syndicate. But it is we three who control the art of the world, and that is why you are here."

"I don't understand."

"Show him the list," Miss Garbo growled.

De Sica produced a sheet of paper and handed it to Muni. "Be good enough to read this list of articles, Professor. Study it carefully. A great deal will depend on the conclusions you draw."

Automatic grill-waffler
Steam-spray iron
12-speed electric mixer
Automatic 6-cup percolator
Electric aluminum fry pan
4-burner gas heater-range w. griddle
11-cubic-foot refrigerator plus 170-lb. freezer
Power sweeper, canister-type, w. vinyl bumper
Sewing machine w. bobbins and needles
Maple-finished-pine wagon-wheel chandelier
Opal-glass ceiling-fixture lamp
Hobnail-glass provincial-style lamp
Pull-down brass lamp w. beaded glass diffuser
Double-bell black-faced alarm clock
50-piece service for 8, mirror-lite flatware
16-piece service for 4, Du Barry-pattern dinnerware
All-nylon pile rug, 9x12, spice beige
Colonial rug, oval, 9x12, fern green
Hemp outdoor "Welcome" mat, 18x30
Sofa-bed and chair, sage green
Round foam-rubber hassock
Serofoam recliner chair w. 3-way mechanism
Drop-leaf extension table, seats 8
4 captain's chairs w. scoop seats
Colonial oak bachelor's chest, 3 drawers
Colonial oak double dresser, 6 drawers
French Provincial canopy bed, 54 in. wide

After studying the list for ten minutes, Professor Muni put the paper down and heaved a deep sigh. "It reads like the most fabulous buried treasure in history," he said.

"Oh, it is not buried, Professor."

Muni sat bolt upright. "You mean these objects actually exist?" he exclaimed.

"Most certainly they do. More of that later. First, have you absorbed the items?"

"Yes."

"You have them in your mind's eye?"

"I do."

"Then can you answer this question: Are these treasures all of a kind, of a style, of a taste?"

"You are obscure, Vittorio," Miss Garbo growled.

"What we want to know," Edward Everett Horton burst out, "is whether one man could —"

"Gently, my dear Horton. Each question in its proper sequence. Professor, perhaps I have been obscure. What I am asking is this: Do these treasures represent one man's taste? That is to say, could the man who — let us say — collected the twelve-speed electric mixer also be the man who collected the hemp outdoor 'Welcome' mat?"

"If he could afford both," Muni chuckled.

"We will, for the sake of argument, say that he can afford all the items on that list."

"A national government couldn't afford all of them," Muni replied. "However, let me think. . . ." He leaned back in his chair and squinted at the ceiling, hardly aware that the Little Group of Powerful Art Dealers was watching him intently. After much face-contorting concentration, Muni opened his eyes and looked around. "Well? Well?" Horton demanded anxiously.

"I've been visualizing those treasures in one room," Muni said. "They go remarkably well together. In fact they would make one of the most impressive and beautiful rooms in the world. If one were to walk into such a room, one would immediately want to know who the genius was who decorated it."

"Then . . . ?"

"Yes. I would say this was the taste of one man."

"Aha! Then your guess was right, Greta. We are dealing with a lone shark."

"No, no, no. It's impossible." Horton hurled his B&B glass into the fire, and then flinched at the crash. "It can't be a lone shark. It must be many men, all kinds, operating independently. I tell you —"

"My dear Horton, pour yourself another drink and calm yourself. You are only confusing the good doctor. Professor Muni, I told you that the items on that list exist. They do. But I did not tell you that we don't know where they are at present. We do not for a very good reason; they have all been stolen."

"No! I can't believe it."

"But yes, plus perhaps a dozen more rarities, which we have not bothered to itemize because they are rather minor."

"Surely this was not a single, comprehensive collection of Americana. I would have been aware of its existence."

"No. Such a single collection never was and never will be."

"Ve vould not permit it," Miss Garbo said.

"Then how were they stolen? Where?"

"By crooks," Horton exclaimed, waving the Brandy & Banana decanter. "By dozens of different thieves. It can't be one man's work."

"The professor has said it is one man's taste."

"It's impossible. Forty daring robberies in fifteen months? I won't believe it."

"The rare objects on that list," De Sica continued to Muni, were stolen over a period of fifteen months from collectors, museums, dealers and importers, all in the Hollywood East area. If, as you say, the objects represent one man's taste —"

"I do."

"Then it is obvious we have on our hands a rara avis, a clever criminal who is also a connoisseur, or, what is perhaps even more dangerous, a connoisseur who has turned criminal."

"But why particularize?" Muni asked. "Why must he be a connoisseur? Any average art dealer could tell a crook the value of antique objets d'art. The information could even be obtained from a library."

"I say connoisseur," De Sica answered, "because none of the stolen objects has ever been seen again. None has been offered for sale anywhere in the four orbits of the world, despite the fact that any one of them would be worth a king's ransom. Ergo, we are dealing with a man who steals to add to his own collection."

"Enough, Vittorio," Miss Garbo growled. "Ask him the next qvestion."

"Professor, we now assume we are dealing with a man of taste. You have seen the list of what he has stolen thus far. I ask you, as a historian: can you suggest any object of virtu that obviously belongs in his collection? If a rare item were to come to his attention, something that would fit in beautifully with that hypothetical room you visualized — what might it be? What would tempt the connoisseur in the criminal?"

"Or the criminal in the connoisseur," Muni added. Again he squinted at the ceiling while the others watched breathlessly. At last he muttered, "Yes . . . Yes . . . That's it. It must be. It would be the focal point of the entire collection."

"What?" Horton cried. "What are you talking about?"

"The Flowered Thundermug," Muni answered solemnly.

The three art dealers looked so perplexed that Muni was forced to elaborate. "It is a blue porcelain *jardinière* of uncertain function, decorated with a border of white and gold marguerites. It was discovered over a century ago by a French interpreter in Nigeria. He brought it to Greece, where he offered it for sale, but he was murdered, and the mug disappeared. It next turned up in the possession of an Uzbek prostitute traveling under a Formosan passport who surrendered it to a quack in Civitavecchia in return for an alleged aphrodisiac.

"The quack hired a Swiss, a deserter from the Vatican Guards, to safeguard him to Quebec, where he hoped to sell the mug to a Canadian uranium tycoon, but he disappeared *en route*. Ten years later, a French acrobat with a Korean passport and a Swiss accent sold the mug in Paris. It was bought by the ninth Duke of Stratford for one million gold francs, and has remained in the Olivier family ever since."

"And this," De Sica asked keenly, "could be the focal point of our connoisseur's entire collection?"

"Most definitely. I stake my reputation on it."

"Bravo! Then our plan is simplicity itself. We much publicize a pretended sale of the Flowered Thundermug to a prominent Hollywood East collector. Perhaps Mr. Clifton Webb is best suited to the role. We much publicize the shipment of the rare treasure to Mr. Webb. We bait a trap in the home of Mr. Webb for our criminal and — Mah! we have him."

"Will the Duke and Mr. Webb cooperate?" Muni asked.

"They will. They must."

"They must? Why?"

"Because we have sold art treasures to both of them, Professor Muni."

"I don't follow."

"My good doctor, sales today are entirely on the residual basis. From five to fifty percent of ownership control and resale value of all works of art remain in our possession. We own residual rights in all those stolen objects too, which is why they must be recovered. Do you understand now?"

"I do, and I see that I'm in the wrong business."

"So. Peter has paid you already?"

"And pledged you to secrecy?"

"I gave my word."

"Grazie. Then if you will excuse us, we have much work to do."

As De Sica handed Muni the coil of rope, binoculars and snub-nosed gun, Miss Garbo said, "No."

De Sica gave her an inquiring glance. "Is there something else, cara mia?"

"You and Horton go and do your vork somevhere else," she growled. "Peter may have paid him, but I have not. Ve vant to be alone." And she beckoned Professor Muni to the bearskin.

In the ornate library of the Clifton Webb mansion on Skouras Drive, Detective Inspector Edward G. Robinson introduced his assistants to the Little Group of Powerful Art Dealers. His staff was lined up before the exquisitely simulated *trompe-l'oeil* book-shelves, and were rather *trompe-l'oeil* themselves in their uniforms of household servants.

"Sergeant Eddie Brophy, footman," Inspector Robinson announced. "Sergeant Eddie Albert, second footman. Sergeant Ed Begley, chef. Sergeant Eddie Mayhoff, second chef. Detectives Edgar Kennedy, chauffeur, and Edna May Oliver, maid."

Inspector Robinson himself was in the uniform of a butler. "Now, ladies and gents, the trap is baited and set, with the invaluable aid of the Police Costume, Prop and Makeup Department, Deputy Commissioner Eddie Fisher in charge, than which there is none better."

"We congratulate you," De Sica said.

"As you very well know," Robinson continued, "everybody believes that Mr. Clifton Webb has bought the Thundermug from Duke Stratford for two million dollars. They are well aware that it was secretly shipped to Hollywood East under armed guard and that at this very moment the art treasure reposes in a concealed safe in Mr. Webb's library." The inspector pointed to a wall, where the combination dial of a safe was artfully set in the navel of a nude by Amedeo Modigliani (2381-2431), and highlighted by a concealed pin spot.

"Vhere is Mr. Vebb now?" Miss Garbo asked.

"Having turned over his palatial mansion to us at your request," Robinson answered, "he is presently on a pleasure cruise of the Carib with his family and servants. As you very well know, this is a closely guarded secret."

"And the Thundermug?" Horton asked nervously. "Where is it?"

"Why, sir, in that safe."

"You mean — you mean you actually brought it over from Stratford? It's here? Oh, my God! Why? Why?"

"We had to have the art treasure transported, Mr. Horton. How else could we have leaked the closely guarded secret to Associated Press, United Television, Reuters News and the Satellite Syndicate, thus enabling them to take sneak photographs?"

"B-but . . . But if it's actually stolen. . . . Oh, my God! This is awful."

"Ladies and gents," Robinson said. "Me and my associates,

the best cops on the Hollywood East force, the Honorable Edmund Kean, Commissioner, will be here, nominally going through the duties of the household staff, actually keeping our eyes peeled, leaving no stone unturned, up to every trick and dodge known in the annals of crime. If anything's taken, it will not be the Flowered Thundermug; it will be the Artsy-Craftsy Kid."

"The who?" De Sica asked.

"Your crooked connoisseur, sir. That's our nickname for him on the Bunco Squad. And now, if you will be good enough to slip out under cover of darkness, using a little-known door in the back garden, me and my associates will begin our simulated domestic duties. We have a hot tip from the underworld that the Artsy-Craftsy Kid will strike — tonight."

The Little Group of Powerful Art Dealers departed under cover of darkness; the Bunco Squad began the evening household routine to reassure any suspicious observer that life was proceeding normally in the Webb pleasance. Inspector Robinson was to be seen, gravely pacing back and forth before the living room windows, carrying a silver salver on which was glued a wineglass, its interior ingeniously painted red to simulate claret.

Sergeants Brophy and Albert, the footmen, alternately opened the front door for each other with much elaborate formality as they took turns going out to mail letters. Detective Kennedy painted the garage. Detective Edna May Oliver hung the bedding out the upstairs windows to air. And at frequent intervals Sergeant Begley (chef) chased Sergeant Mayhoff (second chef) through the house with a meat cleaver.

At 2300 hours, Inspector Robinson put the salver down and yawned prodigiously. The cue was picked up by his staff, and the entire mansion echoed with yawns. In the living room, Inspector Robinson undressed, put on a nightgown and nightcap, lit a candle and extinguished the lights. He put out the library lights, leaving only the pin spot focused on the safe dial. Then he trudged upstairs. In other parts of the house his staff also changed to nightgowns, and then joined him. The Webb home was dark and silent.

An hour passed; a clock chimed twenty-four. A loud clank sounded from the direction of Skouras Drive.

"The front gate," Ed whispered.

"Someone's coming in," Ed said.

"It's the Artsy-Craftsy Kid," Ed added.

"Keep your voices down!"

"Right, Chief."

There was a crunch-crunch-crunch of gravel.

"Coming up the front drive," Ed muttered.

"Oh, he's a deep one," Ed said.

The gravel noises changed to mushy sounds.

"Crossing the flower border," Ed said.

"You got to hand it to him," Ed said.

There was a dull thud, a stumble and an imprecation.

"Stepped into a flowerpot," Ed said.

There came a series of thuddy noises at irregular intervals.

"Can't get it off," Ed said.

A crack and a clatter.

"Got it off now," Ed said.

"Oh, he's slick all right," Ed said.

There came exploratory taps on glass.

"At the library window," Ed said.

"Did you unlock it?"

"I thought Ed was going to do that, Chief."

"Did you, Ed?"

"No, Chief. I thought Ed was supposed to."

"He'll never get in. Ed, see if you can unlock it without him seeing —"

A crash of glass.

"Never mind, he's got it open. You can always trust a pro."

The window creaked up; there were scrapes and grunts as the midnight intruder climbed through When he finally stood upright in the library, his silhouette against the beam of the pin spot was apelike. He looked around uncertainly for some time, and at last began searching aimlessly through drawers and cupboards.

"He'll never find it," Ed whispered. "I told you we should of put a sign under the dial, Chief."

"No, trust an old pro. See? What'd I tell you? He's spotted it. All set now?"

"Don't you want to wait for him to crack it, Chief?"

"Catch him red-handed."

"For God's sake, that safe's burglar proof. Come on now. Ready? Go!"

The library was flooded with light. The thief started back from the concealed safe in consternation, to find himself surrounded by seven grim detectives, all leveling guns at his head. The fact that they were wearing nightshirts did not make them look any less resolute. For their part, the detectives saw a broad-shouldered, bullnecked burglar with a lantern jaw. The fact that he had not altogether shaken off the contents of the flowerpot and wore a Parma violet (Viola pallida plena) on his night shoe, did not make him look any less vicious.

"And now, Kid, if you please," Inspector Robinson said with the exaggerated courtesy that made his admirers call him the Beau Brummel of the Bunco Squad.

They bore the malefactor off to headquarters in triumph.

Five minutes after the detectives departed with their captive, a gentleman in full evening cloak sauntered up to the front door of the Webb mansion. He rang the doorbell. Prom within came the music of the first eight bars of Ravel's Bolero played on full carillon orchestra in waltz tempo. While the gentleman appeared to wait carelessly, his right hand slid through a slit in his cloak and rapidly tried a series of keys in the lock. The gentleman rang the bell again. Midway through the second rendition of the Bolero, he found a key that fitted.

He turned the lock, thrust the door open a few inches with a twist of his toe, and spoke pleasantly, as to an invisible servant inside.

"Good evening. I'm afraid I'm rather late. Is everybody

asleep, or am I still expected? Oh, good. Thank you." The gentleman entered the house, shut the door behind him softly, looked around at the dark, empty foyer, and grinned. "Like taking candy from kids," he murmured. "I ought to be ashamed of myself.

He located the library, entered and turned on all the lights. He removed his cloak, lit a cigarette, noticed the bar and then poured himself a drink from one of the more appealing decanters. He tried it and gagged. "Ack! A new horror, and I thought I knew them all. What the hell is it?" He dipped his tongue into the glass. "Scotch, yes; but Scotch and what?" He sampled again. "My God, it's broccoli juice."

He glanced around, found the safe, crossed to it and inspected it. "Great heavens!" he exclaimed. "A whole three-number dial — all of twenty-seven possible combinations. Absolutely burglar-proof. I really am impressed."

He reached for the dial, looked up, met the nude's melting glance, and smiled apologetically. "I beg your pardon," he said, and began twisting the dial: 1-1-1, 1-1-2, 1-1-3, 1-2-1, 1-2-2, 1-2-3, and so on, each time trying the handle of the safe, which had been cleverly disguised as the nude's forefinger. At 3-2-1, the handle came down with a smart click. The safe door opened, eviscerating, at it were, the lovely belly. The cracksman reached in and brought out the Flowered Thundermug. He contemplated it for a full minute.

A low voice spoke. "Remarkable, isn't it?"

The cracksman looked up quickly. A girl was standing in the library door, examining him casually. She was tall and slender, with chestnut hair and very dark-blue eyes. She was wearing a revealing white sheath, and her clear skin gleamed under the lights.

"Good evening, Miss Webb — Mrs. — ?"

"Miss." She flicked the third finger of her left hand at him.

"I'm afraid I didn't hear you come in."

"Nor I you." She strolled into the library. "You do think it's remarkable, don't you? I mean, I hope you're not disappointed."

"No, I'm not. It's unique."

"Who do you suppose designed it?"

"We'll never know."

"Do you think he didn't make many? Is that why it's so rare?"

"It would be pointless to speculate, Miss Webb. That's rather like asking how many colors an artist used in a painting, or how many notes a composer used in an opera."

She flowed onto a lounge. "Cigarette, please? Are you by any chance being condescending?"

"Not at all. Light?"

"Thank you."

"When we contemplate beauty we should see only the *Ding an sich*, the thing in itself. Surely you're aware of that, Miss Webb."

"I suspect you're rather detached."

"Me? Detached? Not at all. When I contemplate you, I also see only the beauty in itself. And while you're a work of art, you're hardly a museum piece."

"So you're also an expert in flattery."

"You could make any man an expert, Miss Webb."

"And now that you've broken into my father's safe, what next?"

"I intend to spend many hours admiring this work of art."

"Make yourself at home."

"I couldn't think of intruding. I'll take it along with me."

"So you're going to steal it."

"I beg you to forgive me."

"You're doing a very cruel thing, you know."

"I'm ashamed of myself."

"Do you know what that mug means to my father?"

"Certainly. A two-million-dollar investment."

"You think he trades in beauty, like brokers on the stock exchange?"

"Of course. All wealthy collectors do. They buy to own to sell at a profit."

"My father isn't wealthy."

"Oh come now, Miss Webb. Two million dollars?"

"He borrowed the money."

"Nonsense."

"He did." She spoke with great intensity, and her dark blue eyes narrowed. "He has no money, not really. He has nothing but credit. You must know how Hollywood financiers manage that. He borrowed the money, and that mug is the security." She surged up from the lounge. "If it's stolen it will be a disaster for him — and for me."

"Miss Webb, I —"

"I beg you, don't take it. Can I persuade you?"

"Please don't come any closer."

"Oh, I'm not armed."

"You're endowed with deadly weapons that you're using ruthlessly."

"If you love this work of art for its beauty alone, why not share it with us? Or are you the kind of man you hate, the kind that must own?"

"I'm getting the worst of this."

"Why can't you leave it here? If you give it up now, you'll have won a half interest in it forever. You'll be free to come and go as you please. You'll have won a half interest in our family — my father, me, all of us. . . ."

"My God! I'm completely outclassed. All right, keep your confounded —" He broke off.

"What's the matter?"

He was staring at her left arm. "What's that on your arm?" he asked slowly.

"Nothing."

"What is it?" he persisted.

"It's a scar. I fell when I was a child and —"

"That's no scar. It's a vaccination mark."

She was silent.

"It's a vaccination mark," he repeated in awe. "They haven't vaccinated in four hundred years — not like that."

She stared at him. "How do you know?"

In answer he rolled up his left sleeve and showed her his vaccination mark.

Her eyes widened. "You too?"

He nodded.

"Then we're both from . . ."

"From then? Yes."

They gazed at each other in amazement. Then they began to laugh with incredulous delight. They embraced and thumped each other, very much like tourists from the same home town meeting unexpectedly on top of the Eiffel Tower. At last they separated.

"It's the most fantastic coincidence in history," he said.

"Isn't it?" She shook her head in bewilderment. "I still can't quite believe it. When were you born?"

"Nineteen fifty. You?"

"You're not supposed to ask a lady."

"Come on! Come on!"

"Nineteen fifty-four."

"Fifty-four?" He grinned. "You're five hundred and ten years old.

"See? Never trust a man."

"So you're not the Webb girl. What's your real name?"

"Dugan. Violet Dugan."

"What a nice, plain, wholesome sound that has."

"Sam Bauer."

"That's even plainer and nicer. Well!"

"Shake, Violet."

"Pleased to meet you, Sam."

"It's a pleasure."

"Likewise, I'm sure."

"I was a computer man at the Denver Project in seventy-five," Bauer said, sipping his gin and gingersnap, the least horrific combination from the Webb bar.

"Seventy-five?" Violet exclaimed. "That was the year it blew up."

"Don't I know it. They'd bought one of the new IBM 1709's, and IBM sent me along as installation engineer to train the Army personnel. I remember the night of the blast — at least I figure it was the blast. All I know is, I was showing them how to program some new algorisms for the computer when —"

"When what?"

"Somebody put out the lights. When I woke up, I was in a hospital in Philadelphia — Santa Monica East, they call it — and I learned that I'd been kicked five centuries into the future. I'd been picked up, naked, half dead, no identification."

"Did you tell them who you really were?"

"No. Who'd believe me? So they patched me up and discharged me, and I hustled around until I found a job."

"As a computer engineer?"

"Oh, no; not for what they pay. I calculate odds for one of the biggest bookies in the East. Now, what about you?"

"Practically the same story. I was on assignment at Cape Kennedy, doing illustrations for a magazine piece on the first Mars shoot. I'm an artist by trade —"

"The Mars shoot? That was scheduled for seventy-six, wasn't it? Don't tell me they loused it."

"They must have, but I can't find out much in the history books."

"They're pretty vague about our time. I think that war must have wiped most of it out."

"Anyway, I was in the control center doing sketches and making color notes during the countdown, when — well, the way you said, somebody put out the lights."

"My God! The first atomic shoot, and they blew it."

"I woke up in a hospital in Boston — Burbank North — exactly like you. After I got out, I got a job."

"As an artist?"

"Sort of. I'm an antique-faker. I work for one of the biggest art dealers in the country."

"So here we are, Violet."

"Here we are. How do you think it happened, Sam?"

"I have no idea, but I'm not surprised. When you fool around with atomic energy on such a massive scale, anything can happen. Do you think there are any more of us?

"Shot forward?"

"Uh huh."

"I couldn't say. You're the first I ever met."

"If I thought there were, I'd look for them. My God, Violet, I'm so homesick for the twentieth century."

"Me too."

"It's grotesque here; it's all B picture," Bauer said. "Pure Hollywood cliché. The names. The homes. The way they talk. The way they carry on. All like it's straight out of the world's worst double feature."

"It is. Didn't you know?"

"Know? Know what? Tell me."

"I got it from their history books. It seems after that star nearly everything was wiped out. When they started building a new civilization, all they had for a pattern was the remains of Hollywood. It was comparatively untouched in the war."

"Why?"

"I guess nobody thought it was worth bombing."

"Who were the two sides, us and Russia?"

"I don't know. Their history books just call them the Good Guys and the Bad Guys."

"Typical. Christ, Violet, they're like idiot children. No, they're like extras in a bad movie. And what kills me is that they're happy. They're all living this grade Z synthetic life out of a Cecil B. De Mille spectacle, and the idiots love it. Did you see President Spencer Tracy's funeral? They carried the coffin in a full-sized Sphinx."

"That's nothing. Did you see Princess Joan's wedding?"

"Fontaine?"

"Crawford. She was married under anesthesia."

"You're kidding."

"I am not. She and her husband were joined in holy matrimony by a plastic surgeon."

Bauer shuddered. "Good old Great L.A. Have you been to a football game?"

"No."

"They don't play football; they just give two hours of half-time entertainment."

"Like the marching bands; no musicians, nothing but drum majorettes with batons."

"They've got everything air conditioned, even outdoors."

"With Muzak in every tree."

"Swimming pools on every street corner."

"Kleig lights on every roof."

"Commissaries for restaurants."

"Vending machines for autographs."

"And for medical diagnosis. They call them Medicmatons."

"Cheesecake impressions in the sidewalks."

"And here we are, trapped in hell," Bauer grunted. "Which reminds me, shouldn't we get out of this house? Where's the Webb family?"

"On a cruise. They won't be back for days. Where's the cops?"

"I got rid of them with a decoy. They won't be back for hours. Another drink?"

"All right. Thanks." Violet looked at Bauer curiously. "Is that why you're stealing, Sam, because you hate it here? Is it revenge?"

"No, nothing like that. It's because I'm homesick. . . . Try this; I think it's Rum and Rhubarb. . . . I've got a place out on Long Island — Catalina East, I ought to say — and I'm trying to turn it into a twentieth-century home. Naturally I have to steal the stuff. I spend weekends there, and it's bliss, Violet. It's my only escape."

"I see."

"Which again reminds me. What the devil were you doing here, masquerading as the Webb girl?"

"I was after the Flowered Thundermug too."

"You were going to steal it?"

"Of course. Who was as surprised as I when I discovered someone was ahead of me?"

"And that poor-little-rich-girl routine — you were trying to swindle it out of me?"

"I was. As a matter of fact, I did."

"You did indeed. Why?"

"Not the same reason as you. I want to go into business for myself."

"As an antique-faker?"

"Faker and dealer both. I'm building up my stock, but I haven't been nearly as successful as you."

"Then was it you who got away with that three-panel vanity mirror framed in simulated gold?"

"Yes."

"And that brass bedside reading lamp with adjustable extension."

"That was me."

"Too bad; I really wanted that. How about the tufted chaise tongue covered in crewel?"

She nodded. "Me again. It nearly broke my back."

"Couldn't you get help?"

"How could I trust anyone? Don't you work alone?"

"Yes," Bauer said thoughtfully. "Up to now, yes; but I don't see any reason for going on that way. Violet, we've been working against each other without knowing it. Now that we've met, why don't we set up housekeeping together?"

"What housekeeping?"

"We'll work together, furnish my house together and make a wonderful sanctuary. And at the same time you can be building up your stock. I mean, if you want to sell a chair out from under me, that'll be all right. We can always pinch another one."

"You mean share your house together?"

"Sure."

"Couldn't we take turns?"

"Take turns how?"

"Sort of like alternate weekends?"

"Why?"

"You know."

"I don't know. Tell me."

"Oh, forget it."

"No, tell me why."

She flushed. "How can you be so stupid? You know perfectly well why. Do you think I'm the kind of girl who spends weekends with men?"

Bauer was taken aback. "But I had no such proposition in mind, I assure you. The house has two bedrooms. You'll be perfectly safe. The first thing we'll do is steal a Yale lock for your door."

"It's out of the question," she said. "I know men."

"I give you my word, this will be entirely on a friendly basis. Every decorum will be observed."

"I know men," she repeated firmly.

"Aren't you being a little unrealistic?" he asked. "Hero we are, refugees in this Hollywood nightmare; we ought to be helping and comforting each other; and you let a silly moral issue stand between us."

"Can you look me in the eye and tell me that sooner or later the comfort won't wind up in bed?" she countered. "Can you?"

"No, I can't," he answered honestly. "That would be denying the fact that you're a damned attractive girl. But I —"

"Then it's out of the question, unless you want to legalize it; and I'm not promising that I'll accept."

"No," Bauer said sharply. "There I draw the line, Violet. That would be doing it the L.A. way. Every time a couple want a one-night stand they go to a Wedmaton, put in a quarter and get hitched. The next morning they go to a Renomaton and get unhitched, and their conscience is clear. It's hypocrisy! When I think of the girls who've put me through that humiliation: Jane Russell, Jane Powell, Jayne Mansfield, Jane Withers, Jane Fonda, Jane Tarzan — Iyeuch!"

"Oh! You!" Violet Dugan leaped to her feet in a fury. "So,

after all that talk about loathing it here, you've gone Hollywood too."

"Go argue with a woman." Bauer was exasperated. "I just said I didn't want to do it the L.A. way, and she accuses me of going Hollywood. Female logic!"

"Don't you pull your male supremacy on me," she flared. "When I listen to you, it takes me back to the old days, and it makes me sick."

"Violet . . . Violet . . . Don't let's fight. We have to stick together. Look, I'd go along with it your way. What the hell, it's only a quarter. But we'd put that lock on your door anyway. All right?"

"Oh! You! Only a quarter! You're disgusting." She picked up the Flowered Thundermug and turned.

"Just a minute," Bauer said. "Where do you think you're going?"

"I'm going home."

"Then we don't team up?"

"No."

"We don't get together on any terms?"

"No. Go and comfort yourself with those tramps named Jane. Good night."

"You're not leaving, Violet."

"I'm on my way, Mr. Bauer."

"Not with that Thundermug."

"It's mine."

"I did the stealing."

"And I did the swindling."

"Put it down, Violet."

"You gave it to me. Remember?"

"I'm telling you, put it down."

"I will not. Don't you come near me!"

"You know men. Remember? But not all about them. Now put that mug down like a good girl or you're going to learn something else about male supremacy. I'm warning you, Violet. . . . All right, love, here it comes."

* * * *

Pale dawn shone into the office of Inspector Edward G. Robinson, casting blue beams through the dense cigarette smoke. The Bunco Squad made an ominous circle around the apelike figure slumped in a chair. Inspector Robinson spoke wearily.

"All right, let's hear your story again."

The man in the chair stirred and attempted to raise his head. "My name is William Bendix," he mumbled. "I am forty years of age. I am a pinnacle expediter in the employ of Groucho, Chico, Harpo and Marx, construction engineers, at 12203 Goldwyll Terrace."

"What is a pinnacle expediter?"

"A pinnacle expediter is a specialist whereby when the firm builds like a shoe-shaped building for a shoe store, he ties the laces on top; also he puts the straws on top of an ice cream parlor; also he —"

"What was your last job?"

"The Memory Institute at 30449 Louis B. Mayer Boulevard."

"What did you do?"

"I put the veins in the brain."

"Have you got a police record?"

"No, sir."

"What were you perpetrating in the luxurious residence of Clifton Webb on or about midnight last night?"

"Like I said, I was having a vodka-and-spinach in Ye Olde Moderne Beer Taverne — I put the foam on top when we built it — and this guy come up to me and got to talking. He told me all about this art treasury just imported by a rich guy. He told me he was a collector hisself, but couldn't afford to buy this treasury, and the rich guy was so jealous of him he wouldn't even let him see it. He told me he would give a hundred dollars just to get a look at it."

"You mean steal it."

"No, sir, look at it. He said if I would just bring it to the window so he could look at it, he would pay me a hundred dollars."

"And how much if you handed it to him?"

"No, sir, just look at it. Then I was supposed to put it back from whence it come from, and that was the whole deal."

"Describe the man."

"He was maybe thirty years old. Dressed good. Talked a little funny, like a foreigner, and laughed a lot, like he had a joke he wanted to tell. He was maybe medium height, maybe taller. His eyes was dark. His hair was dark and thick and wavy; it would of looked good on top of a barbershop."

There was an urgent rap on the office door. Detective Edna May Oliver burst in, looking distressed.

"Well?" Inspector Robinson snapped.

"His story stands up, Chief," Detective Oliver reported. "He was seen in Ye Olde Moderne Banana Split last night —"

"No, no, no. It was Ye Olde Moderne Beer Taverne."

"Same place, Chief. They just renovated for another grand opening tonight."

"Who put the cherries on top?" Bendix wanted to know. He was ignored.

"This perpetrator was seen talking to the mystery man he described," Detective Oliver continued. "They left together."

"It was the Artsy-Craftsy Kid."

"Yes, Chief."

"Could anyone identify him?"

"No, Chief."

"Damn! Damn! Damn!" Inspector Robinson smote the desk in exasperation. "I have a hunch that we've been tricked."

"How, Chief?"

"Don't you see, Ed? There's a chance the Kid might have found out about our secret trap."

"I don't get it, Chief."

"Think, Ed. Think! Maybe he was the underworld informer who sent us the anonymous tip that the Kid would strike last night."

"You mean squeal on himself?"

"Exactly."

"But why, Chief?"

"To trick us into arresting the wrong man. I tell you, he's diabolical."

"But what did that get him, Chief? You already seen through the trick."

"You're right, Ed. The Kid's plan must go deeper than that. But how? How?" Inspector Robinson arose and began pacing, his powerful mind grappling with the tortuous complications of the Artsy-Craftsy Kid's caper.

"So how about me?" Bendix asked.

"Oh, you can go," Robinson said wearily. "You're just a pawn in a far bigger game, my man."

"No, I mean, can I go through with that deal now? He's prolly still waiting outside the house for a look."

"What's that you say? Waiting?" Robinson exclaimed. "You mean he was there when we arrested you?"

"He must of been."

"I've got it! I've got it!" Robinson cried. "Now I see it all."

"See what, Chief?"

"Don't you get the picture, Ed? The Kid watched us leave with this dupe. Then, after we left, the Kid entered the house."

"You mean . . . ?"

"He's probably there right now, cracking that safe."

"Great Scot!"

"Ed, alert the Flying Squad and the Riot Squad."

"Right, Chief."

"Ed, I want roadblocks all around the house."

"Check, Chief."

"Ed, you and Ed come with me."

"Where to, Chief?"

"The Webb mansion."

"You can't, Chief. It's madness."

"I must. This town isn't big enough for both of us. This time it's the Artsy-Craftsy Kid — or me."

* * * *

It made headlines: how the Bunco Squad had seen through the diabolical plan of the Artsy-Craftsy Kid and arrived at the fabled Webb mansion only moments after he had made off with the Flowered Thundermug; how they had found his unconscious victim, the plucky Audrey Hepburn, devoted assistant to the mysterious gambling overlord Greta "Snake Eyes" Garbo; how Audrey, intuitively suspecting that something was amiss, had taken it upon herself to investigate; how the canny cracksman had played a sinister cat-and-mouse game with her until the opportunity came to fell her with a brutal blow.

Interviewed by the news syndicates, Miss Hepburn said, "It was just a woman's intuition. I suspected something was amiss and took it upon myself to investigate. The canny cracksman played a sinister cat-and-mouse game with me until the opportunity came to fell me with a brutal blow."

She received seventeen proposals of marriage by Wedmaton, three offers of screen tests, twenty-five dollar from the Hollywood East Community Chest, the Darryl P. Zanuck Award for Human Interest and a reprimand from her boss.

"You should also have said you vere ravished, Audrey," Miss Garbo told her. "It vould have improved the story."

"I'm sorry, Miss Garbo. I'll try to remember next time. He did make an indecent proposal."

This was in Miss Garbo's secret atelier, where Violet Dugan (Audrey Hepburn) was busily engaged in faking a calendar of the Corn Exchange Bank for the year 1943, while the members of the Little Group of Powerful Art Dealers consulted.

"Cara mia," De Sica asked Violet, "can you not give us a fuller description of the scoundrel?"

"I've told you everything I can remember, Mr. De Sick The one detail that seems to help is the fact that he computes odds for one of the biggest bookies in the East."

"Mah! There are hundreds of that species. It is no help at all. You did not get a clue to his name?"

"No, sir; at least, not the name he uses now."

"The name he uses now? How do you mean that?"

"I — I meant — the name he uses when he isn't the Artsy-Craftsy Kid."

"I see. And his home?"

"He said somewhere in Catalina East."

"There are a hundred and forty miles of homes in Catalina East," Horton said irritably.

"I can't help that, Mr. Horton."

"Audrey," Miss Garbo commanded, "put down that calendar and look at me."

"Yes, Miss Garbo."

"You have fallen in love vith this man. To you he is a romantic figure, and you do not vant him brought to justice. Is that not so?"

"No, Miss Garbo," Violet answered vehemently. "If there's anything in the world I want, it's to have him arrested." She fingered her jaw. "In love with him? I hate him!"

"So." De Sica sighed. "It is a disaster. Plainly, we are obliged to pay his grace two million dollars if the Thundermug is not recovered."

"In my opinion," Horton burst out, "the police will never find it. They're dolts! Almost as big a pack of fools as we were to get mixed up in this thing in the first place."

"Then it must be a case for a private eye. With our unsavory underworld connections, we should have no difficulty contacting the right man. Are there any suggestions?"

"Nero Volfe," Miss Garbo said.

"Excellent, cara mia. A gentleman of culture and erudition."

"Mike Hammer," Horton said.

"The nomination is noted. What would you say to Perry Mason?"

"That shyster is too honest," Horton snapped.

"The shyster is scratched. Any further suggestions

"Mrs. North," Violet said.

"Who, my dear? Oh, yes, Pamela North, the lady detective. No — no, I think not. This is hardly a case for a woman."

"Why not, Mr. De Sica?"

"There are prospects of violence that make it unsuited to the tender sex, my dear Audrey."

"I don't see that," Violet said. "We women can take care of ourselves."

"She is right," Miss Garbo growled.

"I think not, Greta; and her experience last night proves it."

"He felled me with a brutal blow when I wasn't looking," Violet protested.

"Perhaps. Shall we vote? I say Nero Wolfe."

"Why not Mike Hammer?" Horton demanded. "He gets results, and he doesn't care how."

"But that carelessness may recover the Thundermug in pieces."

"My God! I never thought of that. All right, I'll go along with Wolfe."

"Mrs. North," Miss Garbo said.

"You are outvoted, cara mia. So, it is to be Wolfe, then. Bene. I think we had best approach him without Greta, Horton. He is notoriously antipatico to women. Dear ladies, arrivederci."

After two of the three Powerful Art Dealers had left, Violet glared at Miss Garbo. "Male chauvinists!" she grumbled. "Are we going to stand for it?"

"Vhat can ve do about it, Audrey?"

"Miss Garbo, I want permission to track that man down myself."

"You do not mean this?"

"I'm serious."

"But vhat could you do?"

"There has to be a woman in his life somewhere."

"Naturally."

"Cherchez la femme."

"But that is brilliant!"

"He mentioned a few likely names, so if I find her, I find him. May I have a leave of absence, Miss Garbo?"

"Go, Audrey. Bring him back alive."

* * * *

The old lady wearing the Welsh hat, white apron, hexagonal spectacles, and carrying a mass of knitting bristling with needles, stumbled on the reproduction of the Spanish Stairs, which led to the King's Arms Residenza. The King's Arms was shaped like an imperial crown, with a fifty-foot replica of the Hope diamond sparkling on top.

"Damn!" Violet Dugan muttered. "I shouldn't have been so authentic with the shoes. Sandals are hell."

She entered the Residenza and mounted to the tenth floor, where she rang a hanging bell alongside a door flanked by a lion and a unicorn, which roared and brayed alternately. The door turned misty and then cleared, revealing an Alice in Wonderland with great innocent eyes.

"Lou?" she said eagerly. Then her face fell.

"Good morning, Miss Powell," Violet said, her eyes peering past the lady and examining the apartment.

"I represent Slander Service, Inc. Does gossip give you the go-by? Are you missing out on the juiciest scandals? Our staff of trained mongers guarantees the latest news within five minutes after the event; news defamatory, news derogatory, news libelous, scurrilous, disparaging and vituperative —"

"Flam," Miss Powell said. The door turned opaque.

The Marquise de Pompadour, in full brocade skirt and lace bodice, her powdered wig standing no less than two feet high, entered the grilled portico of Birdies' Rest, a private home shaped like a birdcage. A cacophony of bird calls assailed the ears from the gilt dome. Madame Pompadour blew the bird whistle set in the door, which was shaped like a cuckoo clock. The little hatch above the clock face flew open, and a TV eye popped out with a cheerful "Cuckoo!" and inspected her.

Violet sank into a deep curtsy. "May I see the lady of the house, please?"

The door opened. Peter Pan stood there, dressed ill Lincoln-green transparencies, which revealed her sex.

"Good afternoon, Miss Withers. This is Avon calling. Ignatz

Avon, the Topper Tailor, designs wigs, transformations, chignons, merkins, toupees and hairpieces for fun, fashion and —"

"Fawf," Miss Withers said. The door slammed. The Marquise de Pompadour fawfed.

The Left Bank artiste in beret and velvet smock carried her palette and easel to the fifteenth floor of La Pyramide. Just under the apex there were six Egyptian columns fronting a massive basalt door. When the artiste tossed baksheesh onto a stone beggar's plate, the door swung open on pivots, revealing a gloomy tomb in which stood a Cleopatra type dressed like a Cretan serpent goddess, with serpents to match.

"Good morning, Miss Russell. Tiffany's proudly presents a new coup in organic jewelry, the Tifftoo skin gems. Tattooed in high relief, Tifftoo skin gems incorporate a source of gamma radiation, warranted harmless for thirty days, which outscintillates diamonds of the finest water."

"Shlock!" Miss Russell said. The door closed on its pivots, accompanied by the closing bars of Aida, softly moaned by a harmonica choir.

The schoolmann in crisp tailleur, her hair skinned back into a tight bun, her eyes magnified by thick glasses, carried her schoolbooks across the drawbridge of The Manor House. She was lifted by a crenelated elevator to the twelfth floor, where she was forced to leap across a small moat before she could wield the door knocker, which was shaped like a mailed fist. The door rumbled upward, a miniature portcullis, and there stood Goldilocks.

"Louis?" she laughed. Then her face fell.

"Good evening, Miss Mansfield. Read-Eze offers a spectacular new personalized service. Why submit to the monotony of mechanical readers when Read-Eze experts with cultivated voices, capable of coloring each individual word, will, in person, read you comic books, true-confession and movie magazines at five dollars an hour; mysteries, westerns and society columns at —"

The portcullis rumbled down.

"First Lou, then Louis," Violet muttered. "I wonder."

The little pagoda was set in an exact reproduction of the landscape on a Willow Pattern plate, including the figures of three coolies posed on the bridge. The movie starlet wearing black sunglasses and a white sweater stretched over her forty-four-inch poitrine, patted their heads as she passed.

"That tickles, doll," the last one said.

"Oh, excuse met I thought you were dummies."

"At fifty cents an hour we are, but that's show business."

Madame Butterfly came to the archway of the pagoda, hissing and bowing like a geisha, but rather oddly decorated with a black patch over her left eye.

"Good morning, Miss Fonda. Sky's The Limit is making an introductory offer of a revolutionary concept in bosom uplift. One application of Breast-G, our fleshtinted antigravity powder, under the bust works miracles. Comes in three tints: blond, titian and brunette; and three uplifts: grapefruit, Persian melon and —"

"I don't need no balloon ascension," Miss Fonda said drearily. "Fawf."

"Sorry to have bothered you." Violet hesitated. "Forgive me, Miss Fonda, but isn't that eye patch out of character?"

"It ain't no prop, dearie; it's for Real City. That Jourdan's a bastard."

"Jourdan," Violet said to herself, retracing her steps across the bridge. "Louis Jourdan. Could it be?"

The frogman in black rubber, complete with full scuba equipment including face mask, oxygen tank and harpoon, trudged through the jungle path to Strawberry Hill Place, frightening the chimpanzees. In the distance an elephant trumpeted. The frogman banged on a brazen gong suspended from a coconut palm, and African drums answered. A seven-foot Watusi appeared and conducted the visitor to the rear of the house, where a Pocahontas type was dangling her legs in a hundred-foot replica of the Congo.

"Is it Louis Bwana?" she called. Then her face fell.

"Good afternoon, Miss Tarzan," Violet said. "Up-Chuck, with a fifty-year record of bonded performance, guarantees sterile swimming pleasure whether it's an Olympic pool or just a plain, old-fashioned swimming hole. With its patented mercury-pump vacuum-cleaning system, Up-Chuck chucks up mud, sand, silt, drunks, dregs, debris —"

The brazen gong sounded, and was again answered by drums.

"Oh! That must be Louis now," Miss Tarzan cried. "I knew he'd keep his promise."

Miss Tarzan ran around to the front of the house. Miss Dugan pulled the mask down over her face and plunged into the Congo. On the far side she came to the surface behind a frond of bamboo, alongside a most realistic alligator. She poked its head once to make sure it was stuffed. Then she turned just in time to see Sam Bauer come strolling into the jungle garden, aim in arm with Jane Tarzan.

Concealed in the telephone-shaped booth across the street from Strawberry Hill Place, Violet Dugan and Miss Garbo argued heatedly.

"It vas a mistake to call the police, Audrey."

"No, Miss Garbo."

"Inspector Robinson has been in that house ten minutes already. He vill blunder again."

"That's what I'm counting on, Miss Garbo."

"Then I vas right. You do not vant this — this Louis Jourdan to be caught."

"I do, Miss Garbo. I do! If you'll just let me explain!"

"He captured your fancy vith his indecent proposal."

"Please listen, Miss Garbo. The important thing isn't so much to catch him as it is to recover the stolen loot. Isn't that right?"

"Excuses! Excuses!"

"If he's arrested now, he may never tell us where the Thundermug is."

"So?"

"So we've got to make him show us where it is."

"But how?"

"I've taken a leaf from his book. Remember how he duped a decoy into fooling the police?"

"That stupid creature Bendix."

"Well, Inspector Robinson is our decoy. Oh, look! Something's happening."

Pandemonium was breaking loose in Strawberry Hill Place. The chimpanzees were screaming and flitting from branch to branch. The Watusi appeared, running hard, pursued by Inspector Robinson. The elephant began trumpeting. A giant alligator crawled hastily through the heavy grass. Jane Tarzan appeared, running hard, pursued by Inspector Robinson. The African drums pounded.

"I could have sworn that alligator was stuffed," Violet muttered.

"Vhat vas that, Audrey?"

"That alligator . . . Yes, I was right! Excuse me, Miss Garbo. I've got to be going."

The alligator had risen to its hind legs and was now strolling down Strawberry Lane. Violet left the telephone booth and began following it at a leisurely pace. The spectacle of a strolling alligator followed, at a discreet distance, by a strolling frogman evoked no particular interest in the passers-by of Hollywood East.

The alligator glanced back over his shoulder once or twice and at last noticed the frogman. He quickened his pace. The frogman stayed with him. He began to run. The frogman ran, was outdistanced, turned on her oxygen tank and began to close the gap. The alligator leaped for a handle on the crosstown straphanger and was borne east, dangling from the cable. The frogman hailed a passing rickshaw. "Follow that alligator!" she cried into the hearing aid of the robot.

At the zoo, the alligator dropped off the straphanger and disappeared into the crowd. The frogman leaped out of the rickshaw and hunted frantically through the Berlin House, the Moscow House and the London House. In the Rome House, where sightseers were tossing pizzas to the specimens behind the bars, she saw one of the Romans lying naked and unconscious in a small corner cage. Alongside him was an empty alligator skin. Violet looked around hastily and saw Bauer slinking out, dressed in a striped suit and a Borsalino hat.

She ran after him. Bauer pulled a small boy off an electric carrousel pony, leaped on its back and began galloping west. Violet leaped onto the back of a passing Lama. "Follow that carrousel," she cried. The Lama began running. "Ch-iao hsi-fu nan tso mei mi chou," he complained. "But that's always been my problem."

At Hudson Terminal, Bauer abandoned the pony, was corked in a bottle and jetted across the river. Violet leaped into the coxswain's seat of an eight-oared shell. "Follow that bottle," she cried. On the Jersey side (Nevada East) Violet pursued Bauer onto the Freeway and thence, by Dodge-Em Kar, to Old Newark, where Bauer leaped onto a trampolin and was catapulted up to the forward cylinder of the Block Island & Nantucket Monorail. Violet shrewdly waited until the monorail left the terminal, and then just made the rear cylinder.

Inside, at point of harpoon, she held up a teenage madam and forced her to exchange clothes. Dressed in opera pumps, black net stockings, checked skirt, silk blouse and hair rollers, she threw the cursing madam off the monorail at the blast Vine Street station and began watching the forward cylinder more openly. At Montauk, the eastermost point on Catalina East, Bauer slipped off.

Again she waited until the monorail was leaving the station before she followed. On the platform below, Bauer slid into a Commuters' Cannon and was shot into space. Violet ran to the same cannon, carefully left the coordinate dials exactly as Bauer had set them, and slipped into the muzzle. She was shot off less than thirty seconds after Bauer, and bounced into the landing net just as he was climbing down the rope ladder.

"You!" he exclaimed.

"Me."

"Was that you in the frog suit?"

"Yes."

"I thought I ditched you in Newark."

"No, you didn't," she said grimly. "I've got you dead to rights, Kid."

Then she saw the house.

It was shaped like the house that children used to draw back in the twentieth century: two stories; peaked roof, covered with torn tar paper; dirty brown shingles, half of them hanging; plain windows with four panes in each sash; brick chimney overgrown with poison ivy; sagging front porch; the rotted remains of a two-car garage on the right; a clump of sickly sumac on the left. In the gloom of evening it looked like a haunted house.

"Oh, Sam," she breathed. "It's beautiful!"

"It's a home," he said simply.

"What's it like inside?"

"Come and see."

Inside it was unadulterated mail-order house; it was dime store, bargain basement, second hands castoff, thrift shop, flea market.

"It's sheer heaven," Violet said. She lingered lovingly over the power sweeper, canister-type, w. vinyl bumper. "It's so — so soothing. I haven't been this happy in years."

"Wait, wait!" Bauer said, bursting with pride. He knelt before the fireplace and lit a birch-log fire. The flames crackled yellow and orange. "Look," he said. "Real wood, and real flames. And I know a museum where they've got a pair of matching andirons."

"No! Really?"

He nodded. "The Peabody, at Yale High."

Violet made up her mind. "Sam, I'll help you."

He stared at her.

"I'll help you steal them," she said. "I — I'll help you steal anything you want."

"You mean that, Violet?"

"I was a fool. I never realized. . . . I — You were right. I should never have let such a silly thing come between us."

"You're not just saying that to trick me, Violet?"

"I'm not, Sam. Honest."

"Or because you love my house?"

"Of course I love it, but that's not the whole reason."

"Then we're partners?"

"Yes."

"Shake."

Instead she flung her arms around his neck and pressed herself against him. Minutes later, on the Serofoam recliner chair w. three-way mechanism, she murmured in his ear, "It's us against everybody, Sam."

"Let 'em watch out, is all I have to say."

"And 'everybody' includes those women named Jane."

"Violet, I swear it was never serious with them. If you could see them —"

"I have."

"You have? Where? How?"

"I'll tell you some other time."

"But —"

"Oh, hush!"

Much later he said, "If we don't put a lock on that bedroom door, we're in for trouble."

"To hell with the lock," Violet said.

"*Attention Louis Jourdan*," a voice blared.

Sam and Violet scrambled out of the chair in astonishment. Blue-white light blazed through the windows of the house. There came the excited clamor of a lynch mob, the galloping crescendo of the William Tell Overture, and sound effects of the Kentucky Derby, a 4-6-4 locomotive, destroyers at battle stations, and the Saskatchewan Rapids.

"*Attention Louis Jourdan*," the voice brayed again.

They ran to a window and peered out. The house was surrounded by blinding Kleig lights. Dimly they could see a horde of Jacqueries with a guillotine, television and news cameras, a ninety-piece orchestra, a battery of sound tables manned by technicians wearing earphones, a director in jodhpurs carrying a megaphone, Inspector Robinson at a microphone, and a ring of canvas deck chairs in which were seated a dozen men and women wearing theatrical makeup.

"*Attention Louis Jourdan. This is Inspector Edvard G. Robinson speaking. You are surrounded. We — what? Oh, time for a commercial? All right. Go ahead.*"

Bauer glared at Violet. "So it was a trick."

"No, Sam, I swear it."

"Then what are they doing here?"

"I don't know."

"You brought them."

"No, Sam, no! I — Maybe I wasn't as smart as I thought I was. Maybe they trailed me when I was chasing you; but I swear I never saw them."

"You're lying."

"No, Sam." She began to cry.

"You sold me out."

"*Attention Louis Jourdan. Attention Louis Jourdan. You will release Audrey Hepburn at once*."

"Who?" Bauer was confused.

"Th-that's me," Violet sobbed. "It's the name I took, just like you. Audrey Hepburn and Violet Dugan are one and the s-same person. They think you captured me; but I didn't sell you out, S-Sam. I'm no fink."

"You're leveling with me?"

"Honest."

"*Attention Louis Jourdan. We know you are the Artsy-Craftsy Kid. come out with your hands up. Release Audrey Hepburn and come out with your hands up*."

Bauer flung the window open. "Come and get me, copper," he yelled.

"*Wait until after the network I.D., wise guy*."

There was a ten-second pause for network identification. Then a fusillade of shots rang out. Minuscule mushroom clouds arose where the fission slugs struck. Violet screamed. Bauer slammed the window down.

"Got their ammunition damped to the lowest exponent," he said. "Afraid of hurting the goodies in here. Maybe there's a chance, Violet."

"No! Please, darling, don't try to fight them."

"I can't. I haven't got anything to fight with."

The shots came continuously now. A picture fell off the wall.

"Sam, listen to me," she pleaded. "Give yourself up. I know

it's ninety days for burglary, but I'll be waiting for you when you come out."

A window shattered.

"You'll wait for me, Violet?"

"I swear it."

A curtain caught fire.

"But ninety days! Three whole months!"

"We'll make a new life together."

Outside, Inspector Robinson suddenly groaned and clutched his shoulder.

"All right," Bauer said, "I'll quit. But look at them, turning it into a damned Spectacular — *Gang Busters* and *The Untouchables* and *The Roaring Twenties*. I'm damned if I let them get anything I've pinched. Wait a minute. . . ."

"What are you going to do?"

Outside, the Bunco Squad began coughing, as if from tear gas.

"Blow it all up," Bauer said, rooting around in a sugar canister.

"Blow it up? How?"

"I've got some dynamite I lifted from Groucho, Chico, Harpo and Marx when I was after their pickax collection. Didn't get a pickax, but I got this." He displayed a small red stick with a clockwork top. On the side of the stick was stenciled: TNT.

Outside, Ed (Begley) clutched his heart, smiled bravely and collapsed.

"I don't know how much time the fuse will give us," Bauer said. "So when I start it, go like hell. All set?"

"Y-yes," she quavered.

He snapped the fuse, which began an ominous ticking, and tossed the TNT onto the sage-green sofabed.

"Run!"

They charged out through the front door into the blinding light with their hands up.

The TNT stood for thermonuclear toluene.

"Dr. Culpepper," Mr. Pepys said, "this is Mr. Cristopher Wren. That is Mr. Robert Hooke. Pray, be seated, sir. We have begged you to wait upon the Royal Society and advantage us with your advice as the foremost physician-astrologer in London. However, we must pledge you to secrecy."

Dr. Culpepper nodded gravely and stole a glance at the mysterious basket resting on the table before the three gentlemen. It was covered with green felt.

"Imprimis," Mr. Hooke said, "the articles we shall show you were sent to the Royal Society from Oxford, where they were required of various artificers, the designs for same being supplied by the purchaser. We obtained these specimens from the said craftsmen by stealth. Secundo, the fabrication of the objects was commissioned in secret by certain persons who have attained great power and wealth at the colleges through sundry soothsayings, predictions, auguries and premonstrations. Mr. Wren?"

Mr. Wren delicately lifted the felt cloth as though he feared infection. Displayed in the basket were: a neat pile of soft paper napkins; twelve wooden splinters, their heads curiously dipped in sulphur; a pair of tortoise shell spectacles with lenses of a dark, smoky color; an extraordinary pin, doubled upon itself so that the point locked in a cap; and two large, puffy flannel cloths, one embroidered HIS, and the other, HERS.

"Dr. Culpepper," Mr. Pepys asked in sepulchral tones, "are these the amulets of witchcraft?"

THE END

Printed in Great Britain
by Amazon